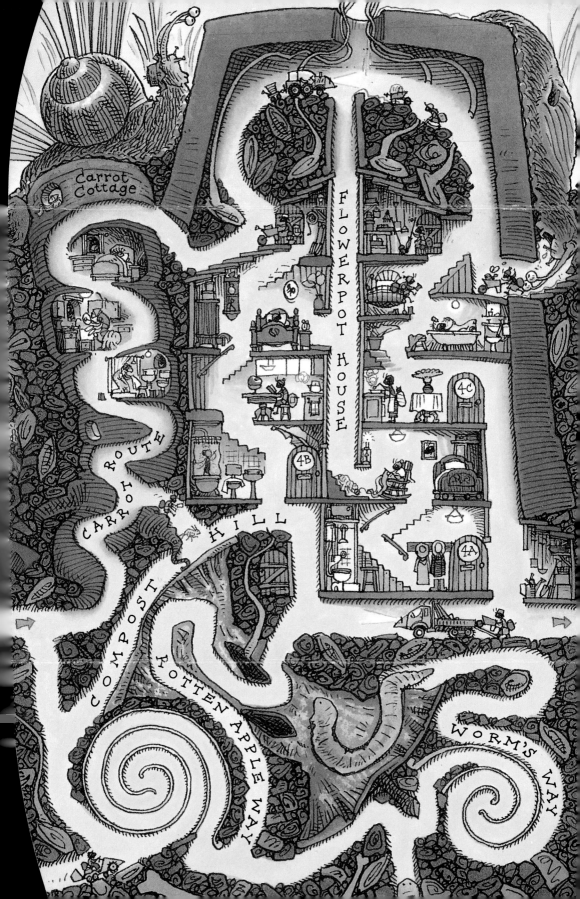

AirMail

To:
Ruby Red Ant
12 Rotten Wood Road
Fungus Farm Estate
Rotten Wood

ROTTEN WOOD LANE

WEEVIL WAY

Weevil Witch Cave

FOSSIL WAY

PEBBLE POOL PASS

ROTTEN WOOD WAY

AirMail

To:
Lucy Woodlouse
Woodlouse House
5 Woodlouse Lane
Rotten Wood

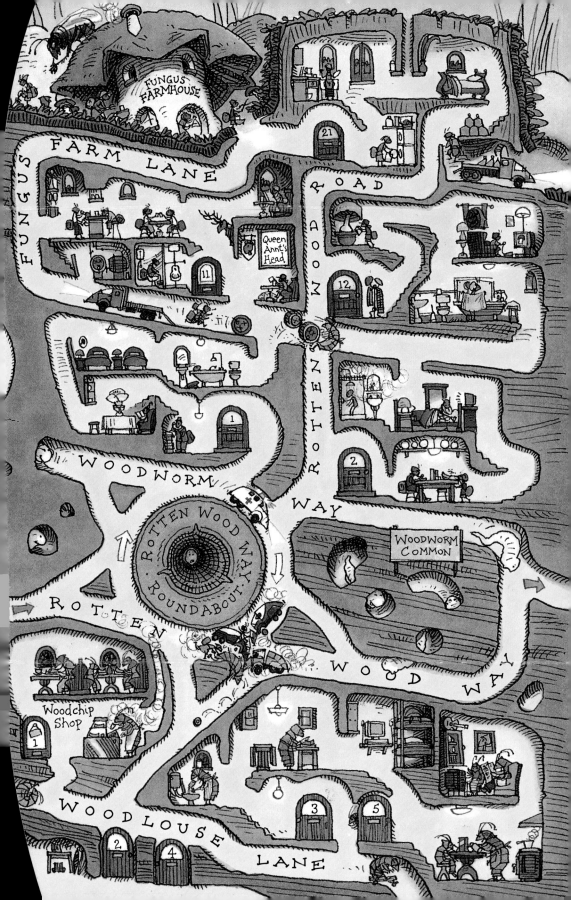

To:
Rocky Ant
c/o RockAnt Climbing Club
Pebble Place
Pebble Mount

AirMail

APHID ALLEY WEST

SPIDER'S PLACE

PEBBLE RISE

BROKEN BONE

BROKEN BONE JUNCTION

BROKEN BONE BEND

PLUMTREE ROUTE

To:
Jeremy Beetle
14 Pebble Pool Parade
Pebble Mount

AirMail